Humpty Dumpty

Daddy is
A Doctor

Jeanette

Doctor Ben

©*Copyright, 1963*

ALLIED PUBLICATIONS, inc.

2485 EAST SUNRISE BLVD., FORT LAUDERDALE, FLORIDA

Library of Congress Catalog Card Number: 63-21268

MANUFACTURED IN THE UNITED STATES OF AMERICA

To

Daddy is

ALLIED PUBLICATIONS, INC., PUBLISHERS

Doctor

Story by Margaret Harold

Illustrated by Mary Richards Gibson

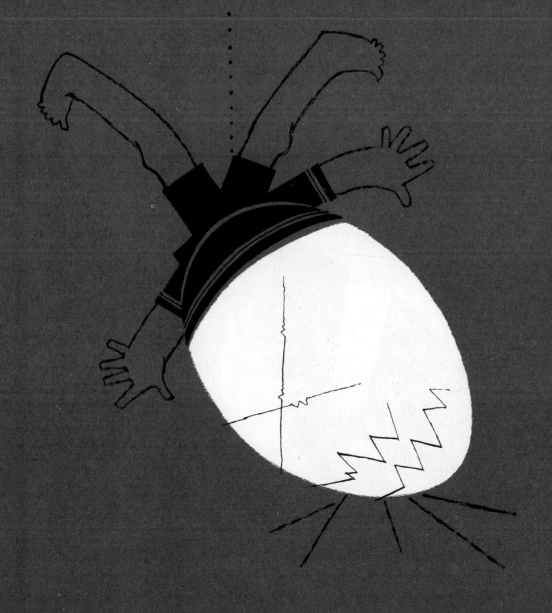

Is YOUR Dad a doctor? Does HE go on calls?
Then you'll like this story and all that befalls.
It's about Humpty Dumpty, Jeanette and Gerard,
Doctor Ben and a dumpy, plump dog named Bernard.
A king and his palace, his horses and men . . .
Well, that's enough preface, so let us begin.

Humpty Dumpty sat high on a wall
Humpty Dumpty had a great fall
All the king's horses
And all the king's men
Couldn't put Humpty together again.

8

"Oh, look at poor Humpty . . . how he's in pain."
Said one of the men as he racked his poor brain.
"Oh who?" cried the horses. "Oh, who?" cried the men.
"Who can put Humpty together again?"
Then one of the horses said "Call Doctor Ben.
He can put Humpty together again."

So off went the horses . . . and off went the men,
And off went the forces to call Doctor Ben.
A horse arrived first . . . and he picked up the phone.
"Doctor Ben, it's the worst," he said with a groan.
"You know Humpty Dumpty? You do, Doctor Ben.
Well, Humpty needs putting together again."

The doctor was playing a game in the yard
With Jeanette and Gerard and their dog named Bernard.
He hung up the phone . . . and he said to the two,
"I MUST go to Humpty's and CANNOT take YOU."
"Oh, please," cried Jeanette. "Oh, please," cried Gerard.
"NOW we won't get our game in the yard."
"But think of poor Humpty and how he's in pain.
Poor Humpty needs putting together again."

11

"Oh, Daddy, don't leave us and spoil all our fun.
Who cares about Humpty?" complained his young son.
"You COULDN'T mean that. You sound like a brat,"
He said with a pat as he put on his hat.

The children ran shouting and chasing their Dad.
(Those two little kids were really quite bad.)
They ran down the driveway right after the car,
And into the highway, but didn't go far.
They stopped and they watched as the car left their sight . . .
Then sat on the curb and pondered their plight.

Then all of a sudden from 'way down the street
A car came and screetched to a stop at their feet.
Two men with cigars invited the two
To jump in the car and go to the zoo.
"We'll buy you some ice cream, some candy and cake.
You'll make no mistake if this ride you will take."
Now both of the children knew well it was wrong
To talk to a stranger . . . much less go along.
Bernard began barking to caution the two:
"Don't go with a stranger. Don't go to the zoo."

14

But both of the children got into the car . . .
Rode off with the men with the big, fat cigar.
"Well, now, little brats, there'll be NO zoo for YOU . . .
For we have decided to barbecue you."
"Oh, please," cried Jeanette. "Oh, please" cried Gerard.
"Oh, please take us back to our dog named Bernard."

By this time the Doctor had reached the big wall
Where poor little Humpty had had a great fall.
The doctor leaned over while all of the men
Watched him put Humpty together again.

The king was so happy he told all his men
"We want to pay homage to great Doctor Ben.
He saved my son's life . . . Prince Humpty the Third.
'Twill be the best banquet I give you my word.
Right here in the palace we'll have a great feast.
So go and tell all . . . from the great to the least."

So off went the horses and off went the men
To tell all the people about Doctor Ben.
"Bring your dog! Bring your wife! Bring your children as well."
Cried the horses and men as they RAN 'round pell-MELL.
The doctor ran home for his wife and his kids,
His dog named Bernard, and his friends, the McGidds.
But when he got home and found BOTH kids were gone,
His wife sitting crying; his dog woebegone . . .

He grabbed his good wife and he ran to the king . . .
"Your Majesty, PLEASE, hear this terrible thing.
My children were kidnapped by two frightful men
While I put poor Humpty together again."

The king called his horses; the king called his men;
The king called his forces to help Doctor Ben.
He sent off his horses; he sent off his men;
He sent off the forces with good Doctor Ben.

Down INto the valley and ALL through the town,

Up over the mountains they hunted aroun'

Then INto a forest with ten thousand trees,

They looked and they searched and they crawled on their knees

Through thickets and thistle, through thick, heavy brush . . .

To find the kids living, they knew they must rush.

Then all of a sudden a terrible thing . . .

That NO one could influence . . . not even the king . . .

It started to rain and it rained more and more
It thundered and lightened as never before.

But just at that moment they happened to see
Two MEN tying KIDS upside DOWN to a TREE!

They looked and they gasped and they grabbed both the men
And sent them away with some guards to the pen.

Then quickly they freed poor Jeanette and Gerard.
(The kids had already begun to breathe HARD).

Then off went the horses and off went the men
With both of the kids of the good Doctor Ben.

The banquet was scheduled for seven that night,
But LONG past eight-thirty not ONE was in sight.

Then all of a sudden the big palace doors
Swung open. And then . . . such commotion! Such roars!
And IN came the people in fours and in scores,
And IN came the horses and IN came the men,
And IN came the forces with good Doctor Ben.

And IN came his wife and his friends, the McGidds,
And IN came a chariot bearing the kids.
And guess who was perched on the lap of Gerard?
You guessed it . . . their dumpy, plump dog named Bernard.

The king gave a talk to Jeanette and Gerard
And juicy, big bones to their dog named Bernard.
On learning the feast was to honor their Dad,
The children were sorry they'd acted so bad.
They really were happy . . . quite happy, you see,
And proud of their Dad . . . an authentic M. D.

'Twas after the dinner and all in the hall . . .
Including poor Humpty who had the great fall . . .
Could hear the king clearing his big, royal throat
Preparing to utter the speech that he wrote.

"My subjects and friends, let's applaud Doctor Ben
And admit that he's great by applauding again."
And all the king's horses and all the king's men
Applauded the doctor again and again.
The king then began to praise Doctor Ben
While all in the hall became quiet again.

"A doctor must study in many fine schools.
In grammar school first where he learns all the rules.
Then high school and college, hard subjects he takes
And studies all day from the time he awakes.
He studies biology, Latin and all,
Plus plenty of others I just can't recall.
But that is not all. No, that is not all"
The king kept repeating to all in the hall.
And all the king's horses and all the king's men
Applauded the doctor again and again.

The king then continued to praise Doctor Ben
While all in the hall became quiet again.

"Then after his college it's medical school,
By that time a doctor is nobody's fool.
Your wonderful body he knows all about,
Completely throughout, therefore inside and out.

"Your bones and appendix, your stomach and throat,
Your lungs and esophagus, PLEASE do take note.
Your heart and its arteries, eyes, ears and nose . . .
Your veins and the blood that flows down to your toes.
Your wonderful body he knows all about
Completely throughout, therefore inside and out.

"But that is not all. No, that is not all,"
The king kept repeating to all in the hall.
And all the king's horses and all the king's men
Applauded the doctor again and again.
The king then continued to praise Doctor Ben
While all in the hall became quiet again.

"A doctor's whole day is spent hearing complaints
From one who can't eat to another who faints.
He goes to the hospital, office, and then
Between times makes visits to sick people when
They're TOO ill to come to his office that day
Or else they've been ordered in bed for a stay.

He works without food 'til you'd think he would drop!
When DO you suppose that the doctor does stop?
He doesn't until he has given a pill
To every last patient who needs it who's ill.

"(Now, children might wonder who 'patients' could be . . .
Well, they are the ones who are ill, don't you see?)

"But let me continue the poor doctor's plight:
Because of his calls he gets home late at night.
Then during his dinner, ding-LING goes the phone,
And over the phone he can hear a big groan.
'Oh, Doctor, Sir, I don't LIKE to complain,
But understand, PLEASE I am feeling great pain.
I've pains in my back and my shoulders and knees . . .
Oh, CAN'T you come over and DO something, please?'

"By this time the doctor has pains of his own.
His stomach needs food. There's an ache in each bone.
His body needs rest . . . and he's yearning to be
At home with his family, as you can well see.
But what is a big-hearted doctor to do?
He can't tell a patient who might have the flu
'I WILL not come out' . . . then bid her adieu.
So what does he do when he hangs up the phone?
You guessed it! He goes out again . . . all alone.

"But that is not all. No, that is not all,"
The king kept repeating to all in the hall.
And all the king's horses and all the king's men
Applauded the doctor again and again.
The king then continued to praise Doctor Ben
While all in the hall became quiet again.

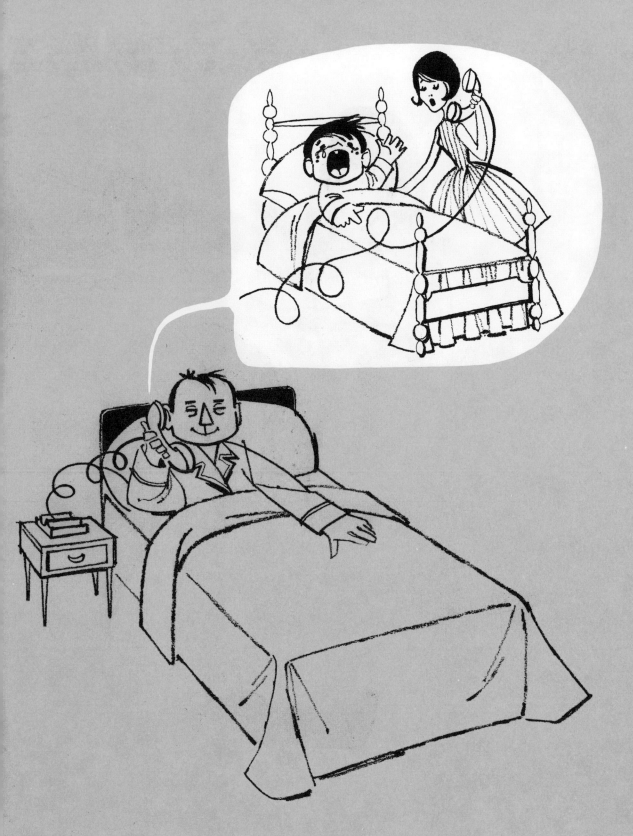

"Now, AS I just told you, a patient might call,
Disturbing his dinner, but that is not all.
Quite often right smack in the still of the night
His sleep is disturbed by a patient in fright.
Her child has a bellyache, fever and cough . . .
There's nothing to do, but to go. So he's off.

"But that is not all. No that is not all,"
The king kept repeating to all in the hall.

"It's hard to believe, but there comes a gay day
When doctors do finally get time off to play.
It might be a game in the yard with his kids
Or a fun-funny party at his friends', the McGidds.
But then . . ."

47

Then all of a sudden a very odd thing . . .
A messenger came with a note for the king.
The king donned his specs to see WHAT the boy WROTE,
While all in the hall shouted "WHAT'S in that NOTE?"
The king then uplifted his big, royal hand
As if he were giving a great, big command.
"Emergency call for the great Doctor Ben,"
He read. Then he read it again and again . . .
While all in the hall simply moaned a loud groan.
But poor Doctor Ben quickly went to the phone.

Returning, he bade all the people good night,
And thanked the good king for a banquet delight.

Then asked that his car be brought up to the door
And gathered his fam-i-ly . . . one, two, three, four.

They drove down the avenue into the night . . .
And watched as the palace was lost from their sight.
They heard the king SAY, "Let's applaud Doctor Ben
And admit that he's great by applauding again."

They heard the king's horses and heard the king's men
Applauding the doctor again and again.

Gerard then looked up, and he said to his Dad,
"A doctor's the best Dad a lad ever had."
Jeanette then began to applaud Doctor Ben
And both, then, applauded again and again.

54

The kids and their Mother were swelled with great pride
As they rode down the avenue right by his side.

They really were happy and proud, don't you see . . .
As YOU should be TOO if your DAD's an M.D.!!!

Titles in this series are as follows:

Daddy is a Doctor

Daddy is a Dentist

Daddy is an Accountant

Daddy is a Salesman

Daddy is a Banker

Daddy is a Clergyman

Daddy is an Executive

Daddy is a Teacher

Daddy is a Lawyer

Daddy is an Architect

Daddy is a Merchant

Daddy is a Manufacturer

Daddy is a Distributor

Daddy is an Engineer

Daddy is a Golfer

Daddy is a Fisherman

Daddy is an Artist

and many more

all the kings horses and all the king

The King

Mummy

Gerard

Bernard